STILL IN THE GAME?

The Hornets had two timeouts left and a little less than two minutes to work with. But they also had eighty-two yards to go.

Jason called a play that targeted Calvin as the receiver fifteen yards upfield near the sideline. "Preserve the clock," he said. "Get out of bounds if you can."

He took the snap and stepped back into the pocket, but the defenders were already closing in. Anthony and Sergio and the others were battling to give Jason protection, but white-uniformed arms were reaching high to thwart any passes and the red-uniformed Hornets were being driven backwards.

Jason darted to his left and managed to escape from the horde, but a linebacker brought him down after a three-yard gain. . . . More importantly, the clock was still running.

Winning Season Series

Double Fake

Emergency Quarterback

The Roar of the Crowd

Technical Foul

WINNING SEASON

RICH WALLACE

SCHOLASTIC INC.
New York Toronto London Auckland Sydney
Mexico City New Delhi Hong Kong Buenos Aires

ISBN-13: 978-0-439-89566-8
ISBN-10: 0-439-89566-9

Published by Scholastic Inc., 557 Broadway, New York, NY 10012, by arrangement with Puffin Books, a member of Penguin Group (USA) Inc.

12 11 10 9 8 7 7 8 9 10 11/0

Printed in the U.S.A. 40

First Scholastic printing, October 2006

Set in Caslon 224 Book

FOR MOM AND DAD

EMERGENCY QUARTERBACK

• CONTENTS •

1

Fingertips

Jason Fiorelli lined up at wingback and scanned the opponents' defense. He wiped his hands on his muddy jersey as he glanced at the scoreboard: fourth quarter, 1:39. Time was running out. The Hudson City Hornets trailed, 14–7.

Quarterback Vinnie DiMarco called the signals, and Jason exhaled hard. He wanted the ball. The glare of the lights, the smell of wet grass, the tension in the bleachers and on the field—this was crunch time.

Shoulder pads collided as the ball was snapped, and Jason held his ground, waiting for the rush of defenders. A linebacker burst through the seam and Jason threw a glancing block that barely slowed him down. But that was the whole idea.

Jason drifted to his left as another defender scooted into the backfield. Perfect. The field was wide open.

And here came DiMarco's screen pass, lofting gently toward Jason above the on-rushing defenders. He felt the almost weightless solidity of the football as it settled into his hands. And with that lightning-quick acceleration that made him such a dangerous receiver, Jason reached full speed in an instant and streaked up the field toward the end zone.

He had blockers at his side but he didn't need them, racing along the sideline. His arm muscles were flexed as he cradled the ball against his chest, and his breathing was hard but steady as he put all his might into every stride.

His cleats gripped the slippery grass and every step got him closer. A frustrated cornerback made a futile dive at the ten-yard line, but Jason was out of reach. Touchdown!

He raised his fist and resisted the temptation to slam the ball into the ground, tossing it to an official instead and leaping into the arms of teammate Miguel Rivera. "Did it, man!" Jason yelled. "Got that ball and I was *gone*."

He looked up at the bleachers, expecting a wild ovation. But while the Hudson City fans were on their feet, most were staring out at the center of the field, where officials and coaches were huddled around a fallen player.

"What happened?" Jason asked.

"DiMarco got nailed," Miguel said. "You didn't hear the crunch?"

"Didn't hear nothing."

"You must've been running faster than sound. That hit was *intense*."

Players from both teams were circling around now, and the coaches were motioning for them to stay back. DiMarco had his helmet off and Jason could see that he was conscious, but he was lying flat on the field and his face was set in a grimace.

Jason stepped over to an assistant coach. "Knee?" he asked.

"Wrist," said the coach, slowly shaking his head. "He got clobbered."

It took several minutes before Vinnie was helped off the field. He waved to the crowd with his left hand but walked slowly along the running track toward the locker room, accompanied by a small group of adults.

Coach Podesta called the offense over. "Listen up," he said with a stern expression. "Vinnie will be all right. We still have a game to win here. Everybody with me?"

Several players nodded. With all the confusion and delay, Jason had nearly forgotten that they hadn't even tied the score yet. South Bergen still had a 14–13 lead.

"We have to go for two points," Coach said. "We don't have another kicker that I trust under pressure."

The head referee had walked over. "Coach," he said, "let's get that team on the field."

Coach nodded. "Wade, get the ball to Jason. Let's go."

DiMarco had not only been the quarterback,

he was also the Hudson City placekicker. So the Hornets couldn't go for the tie even if they wanted to. Instead, they'd try for a two-point conversion and a win. Wade Brigham would be at quarterback for the most crucial play of the year. The team's unbeaten record was in jeopardy.

Jason grabbed the sleeve of Wade's jersey and stared up at the quarterback's pale eyes. "Don't be a hero," Jason said sternly, well aware of Wade's tendency to run with the ball. "I'm doing a simple square-out in the flat. Get the pass near me and I'll catch it."

Wade didn't say a thing. He just walked to the huddle, called the play Jason had insisted on, and lined up with the rest of the team.

Now the spectators were yelling. A South Bergen linebacker glared across at Jason, and the cornerback was coiled a few yards behind him. They knew where the ball was going.

Jason darted from the line and was met with a fierce shove by the linebacker. He stumbled but found his feet, feinting toward the center of the field, then charging toward the corner of the end zone.

He was open, but Wade wasn't even looking his way. Instead he threw a wobbly pass in the direction of tight end Lamont Wilkins.

Jason changed direction and sprinted toward the ball. A linebacker batted at it, and it flipped wildly into the air, out of Lamont's reach.

Jason had a chance. He dove headlong toward the ball, extending both arms in front of him and lifting his head to avoid ramming his face mask into the turf. He got the fingertips of his right hand below the ball, flicking it slightly toward him and cradling it with his left. He held on.

There was the whistle, the referee extending his arms above his head to signal a score. Two points. Hudson City had the lead!

Lamont and Miguel and big Anthony Martin all fell on top of Jason, smothering him in their joy.

"Incredible catch!" Miguel shouted. "It must be your birthday or something!"

"You are *the man*!" cried Anthony.

Jason trotted to the sideline and drank it all in. The cheerleaders were leaping and yelling, and the red-clad fans of the Hudson City Hornets were standing in the bleachers, pumping their fists and cheering.

The final minute was a blur to him: the kickoff, some long incomplete passes, Anthony's massive sack of the South Bergen quarterback. When it ended, Coach Podesta lifted Jason in a bear hug. "You're the best player I've ever coached," he said. "That catch was amazing. I've never seen anything like it."

2

What's Next?

Players were whooping in the locker room, celebrating the comeback victory as they pulled off their shoulder pads and cleats. Jason shared in the fun, his face set in that wicked half-smile of his that always seemed to be on the verge of laughter. But he had a nagging feeling that things were about to change. Vinnie was nowhere to be seen.

Coach came in and rapped his fist gently on a locker to get the team's attention. "Great win," he said, but his face was serious. "Vinnie's been examined, and it looks like that wrist may be broken. And even if it's only a bad sprain, there's not much chance he'll be ready to play again this season. There are only three games left."

Jason looked around at his teammates' shocked faces as Coach gave the grim news. But then his eyes fixed on Wade, who seemed to be fighting back a smile. He'd be getting back the first-string quarterback job he felt he deserved.

What a jerk, Jason thought.

Jason had taken off his shoulder pads, so his red jersey hung loosely around his wiry frame. He grabbed his pads, helmet, and cleats and stepped outside, looking for his mom and dad. There was a cold, empty feeling in his gut.

"Great game," said Mr. Fiorelli, patting Jason on the back. He was a tall man, very athletic like his son. They had the same wavy, wheat-colored hair, but Mr. Fiorelli's was cut much shorter than Jason's and was thinning on top.

Jason nodded. His mouth was set in a tight line, a big contrast to his usual easygoing expression.

The DiMarco-Fiorelli passing combination was a huge reason the team was undefeated. Now, whiny Wade would either steal some of that glory or waste it.

"We're in trouble," Jason said. "Vinnie's through."

"Don't think that way," Dad said. "Somebody will step up."

"Maybe. . . . We'll see."

"You must be starving."

"Not really."

"You will be. You can get a sandwich at home."

"Okay if I go out instead? Me and Anthony and some others were gonna get tacos or something."

"As long as you don't stay out too late," said his mom. She was also an athlete—a tennis player and runner. "Here's your jacket."

"I'm not cold, Mom. And I'm not even hungry. I just need to talk to the guys. Figure out what to do about the quarterback situation."

Mrs. Fiorelli laughed. "I think the coaches will figure that one out. Besides, Wade was the starter a year ago. He'll be fine."

Jason rolled his eyes. "They won *two games* last season. Wade's terrible."

"He's the best you've got," Mrs. Fiorelli said.

"That's not saying much."

Anthony and Miguel had walked over. "Ready for some fine dining?" asked Anthony, a powerful lineman with a round, brown face and a wide smile.

"Very ready," Jason replied. "Let's go."

They walked up to El Torito, a small Mexican restaurant on the Boulevard that was run by Miguel's uncle. They took a booth by the front window and snacked on salsa and chips while they waited for their tacos to arrive.

"Still can't believe it," Miguel said, wiping spicy sauce from the corner of his mouth with his thumb. He had intense, dark eyes and the slightest beginnings of a mustache sprouting above his lip. "Biggest game of the year is next week and we're stuck with Wade again."

Wade was an eighth-grader, a year ahead of Jason and his friends. He'd been the starting quarterback for the seventh-and-eighth-grade team the year before, when Vinnie DiMarco was leading the fifth-and-sixth-graders.

Vinnie had consistently outplayed Wade during summer training camp this year, so it was no surprise to anyone but Wade when Coach Podesta named Vinnie as the starter a few days before the first game. Vinnie had proven that the coach made the right decision by leading the team to five straight wins. But now his season was over.

Jason stared glumly out the window. Anthony gave him a light smack on the arm. "Hey!" he said. "We *won*. You look like we got clobbered."

Jason just nodded. Words usually poured out of his mouth in an energetic, joking stream. But not tonight.

"Show me the hand," Anthony said firmly.

"What?"

"The hand. The one that made that famous, one-handed, game-winning grab."

Jason fought back a smile. He spread out the fingers of his left hand and held it over the table.

"That's the one!" Anthony said. "Oooooh. That's something."

Jason laughed now and pulled back his hand.

"No," Anthony said. "Hold it up. Let everybody see."

A waitress walked by carrying a tray of food. She glanced at the boys.

"Look at this hand!" Anthony said to her, grabbing Jason by the wrist and holding it up. "He's got glue on his fingers or something. Or else it really *is* his birthday. The boy can catch anything. Throw that tray of food over here. He won't spill a drop."

The waitress smiled and shook her head.

"Throw him a fork, at least. He'll catch it."

Jason pulled his hand out of Anthony's grasp and turned to face his friend head-on. "Shut up," he said playfully. "And it ain't my birthday."

Anthony poked Jason in the chest with a finger. "We're undefeated. We can win without Vinnie."

"I know."

"Vinnie wasn't in there for the game-winning play."

"I know."

"Wade was."

"I know. . . . But Wade threw the lamest pass

of the year. It wasn't anywhere near me."

"You got to it."

"I know."

"Repeat after me," Anthony said, reciting one of the cheerleaders' most common riffs. "'T-E-A-M. Yaaay *team*.' We lost *one* guy. We're too good to let that stop us."

Anthony said he needed to use the restroom. When he came back, he was obviously trying to suppress a laugh.

"What?" Jason asked.

"Nothing." But it soon become clear what he was laughing about. The sounds of "Happy Birthday" came over from the jukebox, and he and Miguel started singing. When the song reached "Happy birthday, dear . . ." there was only music instead of the name, so they provided it: "Jason!"

Jason just shook his head slowly with an embarrassed grin. "It's not my birthday," he said over and over.

Jason's parents were reading the newspaper at the

kitchen table the next morning when he came down for breakfast. He was wearing baggy gray gym shorts and a red T-shirt that said HORNET PRIDE.

"Can I have the sports section?" he asked.

He flipped quickly through the pages of professional and high-school sports coverage, finding the youth sports section on page 7. He scanned the standings for the East Jersey Junior Football League (which everybody referred to as the E–Double-J–F–L).

	W	L	T	Pct.
Hudson City	5	0	0	1.000
Bayonne	3	1	1	.750
Hoboken	3	1	1	.750
Liberty	4	2	0	.667
West Newark	2	2	1	.500
South Bergen	2	4	0	.333
Arlington	1	3	1	.250
Greenville	1	4	0	.200
Palisades	1	5	0	.167

Saturday's scores:
Liberty 23, West Newark 21
Hudson City 15, South Bergen 14
Arlington 13, Palisades 7
Hoboken 27, Greenville 6

Next week:
Liberty at Hoboken
South Bergen at Arlington
Bayonne at Hudson City
Greenville at West Newark

With three games left, Hudson City was very much in control of its destiny. But Bayonne would be the toughest test yet, and then, after a game with Palisades, the Hornets would end the season against Hoboken. Hoboken had won the title three out of the past four seasons. Hudson City hadn't won it in twenty years. In fact, the town had won very few titles in any sport. Jason was determined to change all that.

Ever since he'd learned to read he had been checking out the sports section, dreaming that one day he'd see a photo of himself there, with a big headline like *Fiorelli Leads Hornets to Title* or *Hudson City Triumphs Behind Fiorelli.* Of course, youth sports rarely made the headlines; it was all professional, collegiate, or high school. And even though he was too young to do anything about it yet, it bothered him that the high-school headlines were usually along the lines of *Bayonne Stomps Hudson City* or *Hornets Stung by Hoboken.*

But he knew a change was coming. His class—the seventh-graders led by himself, DiMarco, Miguel, and the others—was building a tradition of winning. Last winter, Jason had been a starter for the Hudson City Middle School basketball team that won the league crown. And here they were again, undefeated in football.

Jason was leading the league in total number of receptions (27), touchdown receptions (6), and scoring. In addition to the six touchdown catches, he'd scored on a running play and a punt return. Last night's two-point conversion gave him fifty points for the season.

He was the type of athlete who always made things happen. Whether it was basketball, football, or just a pickup game of hockey on the playground, he was in the center of the action. Usually he came out as a winner—he had great natural ability, and observers often commented that his performances on the field or on the court seemed effortless.

He picked up the phone and dialed Vinnie's number. "Hey, Mrs. DiMarco," Jason said when she answered. "Good news or bad?"

"Not great," she said. "It's not a bad break, so it should heal fine. But it'll take a while. You want to talk to him?"

"Yeah."

It was several minutes before Vinnie picked up. He sounded tired and far away.

"How you doing?" Jason asked.

"Okay, I guess."

"We won."

"I heard. That's a relief."

"You threw the winning touchdown pass."

Vinnie gave a short, grunting laugh. "I paid for it, too. As soon as I let go of the ball, I got drilled."

"Well, it was a good pass."

"Last one for this season."

"I know," Jason said. "We're dead."

"No you ain't."

"How do you figure?"

"Wade can handle it. He started last year. He almost started *this* year."

"No way. It wasn't even close."

"Closer than you think. He's not *that* bad. You guys just have to work on him. He's selfish and he plays it too safe, but he can throw the ball if the line just gives him some time."

"I don't know," Jason said. It was probably true that the team could continue winning, but the individual honors mattered to him, too. He needed to catch a lot more passes if he was going to lead the league in receiving.

But without Vinnie throwing the ball, how many more receptions would he get? Winning the championship probably depended on that number.

"We need you badly," he said.

"Ain't gonna happen," Vinnie said. "Just hang in there. The worst thing you could do is give up now."

3

Scrambling Man

Jason jogged across the practice field Monday afternoon, out of breath from another long, fruitless sprint along the sideline. He'd been open, but Wade hadn't even looked his way. Instead, he'd been sacked in the backfield trying to carry the ball himself.

"Where was the pass?" Jason said to the tall, awkward quarterback as they huddled up.

"You took too long to get open," Wade said, looking away. "They were all over me."

"I've got my man beat," Jason said. "Every play. Just get the ball to me."

"*I'm* in charge here," Wade said, shaking his head. He kneeled among the offensive players. "Eighty-three," he said, calling for a long-pass play. He glanced up at Jason, then looked straight ahead. "On three. Let's go."

Jason spread out wide to the left, nearly to the sideline. Cornerback Calvin Tait took a few steps in toward Jason, then stepped back. Calvin was fast, but Jason was hard to contain.

Wade lined up in a shotgun position, several yards back from the center. He called signals and fielded the snap, dropping back and looking toward the sideline.

Jason sprinted out from the line and Calvin wheeled around to stay with him. The play called for Jason to simply outrun the defender, but Calvin had him covered well. So Jason gave a quick hesitation—forcing Calvin to stutter—and cut back toward the center of the field, a couple of steps in the clear.

And here came the football, but it soared way over Jason's head and landed on the sideline.

Jason stood and stared at the ball. It hadn't

come close. Wade hadn't completed a single pass to him all afternoon.

"What was that?" he said as he got back to the huddle.

"That was right where you were supposed to be," Wade said sharply. "That's the play."

"But I wasn't there! You ever hear of an adjustment? Calvin was on my butt so I changed the pattern."

"I threw the ball where I was supposed to."

"This ain't a video game! I was wide open in the middle of the field. You didn't see me?"

"I saw you running the wrong pattern."

"So you threw it anyway?"

"I threw it where the play was designed to go."

"You're an idiot."

Miguel put his hand on Jason's chest and stepped between him and the quarterback. "Suck it up," Miguel said. He turned to Wade. "You made your point, okay? But don't throw the ball away to spite your own teammate."

Wade just shrugged and called a play. He threw another incomplete pass, this time on the side of the field away from Jason.

The scrimmage proceeded that way for several minutes, with the defense dominating and the offensive players beginning to squabble in the huddle even more.

Coach Podesta had been watching quietly, letting the players try to work things out for themselves. He believed that a bit of tension and even some hot tempers in practice were not always bad things. Smart players would learn to work together.

But Wade was clearly not doing much of a job leading the team. Coach had hoped that, given another shot to play, Wade would be ready to overcome the ego that had thwarted him the season before.

Eventually, Coach sent in substitutes for Jason and Sergio Guzman, the starting center.

"What's up?" Jason asked as he reached the sideline.

"Start taking some snaps from Sergio," Coach said. "I was hoping Wade could grow up, but I think I know what we have to do."

"You're putting me at quarterback?" Jason asked in disbelief.

"I want to give it a try," Coach said. "We need a great athlete out there. A leader. Take a few practice snaps and we'll see what you can do."

"I've never played quarterback."

"You know all the plays. You've got the skills. Let's try it."

Jason took a deep breath and wiped his sweaty hands on his pants. Sergio held up a ball and gave Jason a grin. "Football," he said, twirling the ball around. "It's very simple. I hike the ball to you, then I get hit by that ten-ton truck named Anthony. All he wants to do is run me over, chase you down, and make you eat this little ball. You've got three-tenths of a second to react. Have fun."

Jason took several snaps. An assistant coach showed him how to hold his hands to receive the ball, how to back up in a hurry, and how to make a proper handoff to a running back.

"Okay," Coach Podesta said after a few minutes. "Let's get out there."

Coach blew his whistle and walked onto the

field with Jason and Sergio right behind him. "Take a break, Wade," Coach said. "Fellas, we can't afford to have only one tested quarterback, so Jason is going to be our emergency man. We're switching to a tightly controlled scrimmage—no sacking the new QB. If you hear my whistle, stop running. That means you, Anthony."

"Can I give him a bear hug instead of tackling him?" Anthony asked.

"A gentle one."

Coach joined the offensive players in the huddle. "Thirty-three," he said. "That's a handoff to the fullback between the left guard and tackle, right, Jason?"

"Right," Jason replied. "On two. Let's go."

Coach walked away, and Jason lined up behind Sergio. "Ready. Set. Hut. Hut." Jason felt the ball strike his fingers, and he pulled back quickly, nearly dropping it. He had it by his fingertips, a poor grip, and he turned and held it out for fullback Jared Owen. But Jared was wider out than Jason expected, and he had to lunge to get it to him.

The ball hit Jared's hip and slipped to the

ground. It bounced awkwardly and Jason tried to dive for it, but he was roughly pushed aside. When the whistle blew, Anthony was on top of the ball, shielding it with his large arms and shoulders.

"Sorry," Jason said as they huddled up.

"Try it again," Coach said. "Same play. Let's get it right."

This time Jason took the snap cleanly and did a better job of handing off to Jared, who forced his way forward for three yards.

Coach called a couple of pass plays, and Jason completed the second one to Lamont, a short bullet over the middle. Then he fumbled another snap, but he was able to fall on the ball just ahead of Anthony, who smothered him.

"Those famous fingers aren't working so good," Anthony said as he pulled Jason to his feet.

"I'll get there," Jason replied. He was nervous, but he was starting to like the new position.

Calvin Tait had switched over to offense, taking Jason's spot at wingback. "Let's run that fly pattern," Coach said. "You know it, Calvin—you've covered Fiorelli enough times."

Jason lined up in the shotgun. He took the snap and drifted toward Calvin's side of the field, watching for just the right second to unload the pass. But Anthony was already in pursuit, and linebacker Anderson Otero was circling toward him as well. Calvin was tightly covered. This wasn't going to work.

Jason pivoted and ran wide around Anthony, scrambling toward the other side of the field. He was twelve yards behind the line of scrimmage, in danger of a huge loss if he was caught. But his speed carried him past the on-rushing linemen, and suddenly he was heading upfield, going wide around the end and cutting along the sideline.

The field was clear ahead of him, but Willie Shaw was racing over from his cornerback position, and the angle between them was to Willie's advantage. Jason upped his speed another notch, tucking in the ball and sprinting. Willie dove and Jason leaped, feeling Willie's hand slip off his calf. Jason landed hard, caught his balance, and ran unchallenged into the end zone.

Jason trotted back. Coach had called all of the

players together, and they were standing near him or kneeling with their helmets off.

"That's what I was looking for," Coach said. "Without Vinnie in there, we need to adjust in a big way. Jason hasn't got the experience, but he's certainly got the athleticism."

"You've got to be kidding me!" came Wade's voice. Everyone turned to look at him.

"*I'm* the quarterback," Wade said. "You said he was just the emergency guy."

"That's right," Coach replied.

"Sounds like you're planning to switch to him."

"I haven't made that decision yet," Coach said. "But Jason's got the talent we need. Your status hasn't changed, Wade. We need you. But we need to explore all the options. We've got a championship to win."

4

The Starting QB

A group of people were clustered near Jason's school locker as he approached the next morning. Jason smiled as he saw why. Vinnie DiMarco was back in school—his right wrist in a heavy cast and the arm in a sling.

Jason gently pushed through and gripped his friend's good arm. Vinnie grinned back. He was a hard worker and always had a good attitude—win or lose. It didn't seem fair to Jason that his buddy could get such a rotten break when they were on the verge of a title.

"How's the pain?" Jason asked.

"Comes and goes. I can stand it."

"Bad timing, brother."

"Yeah. Heard you might be the backup."

Jason rolled his eyes. "Looks like it. Too bad I can't pass to myself."

"At least you'd get your hands on the ball."

"Yeah. Wade never passes to me if he can help it."

Vinnie looked around before speaking. Everybody there—Anthony, Miguel, Lamont, Willie—were his allies. "Wade's been a jerk," Vinnie said, "but part of it was because I took away his job. And he's jealous of you for being the star. Anyway, he's got the job back now. So give him a chance to lead."

"Some leader," Jason replied. "Wade couldn't lead a herd of sheep."

The bell rang for homeroom and the boys started to leave. "Wait," Jason said to Vinnie. "You coming to practice?"

"Nothing else to do," Vinnie said with a shrug. "I'll be cheering."

"Can you kick?"

Vinnie looked surprised. He thought for a moment. "I don't think they'd let me. But maybe." He planted his left foot and swung his right as if kicking a ball. "Feels a little awkward with this arm tied up, but I think I could do it. Maybe something short, like an extra point."

"That would be great."

Vinnie shrugged. "My parents would have a fit. Doctor probably would, too. . . . We'll see."

Jason hustled away toward his homeroom. Vinnie was part of the new attitude and outlook he wanted so badly to bring to Hudson City sports. In Jason's mind, Wade was a symbol of that old era of consistent losing—last season's 2–6 record being all the evidence he needed.

Now, with Vinnie on the sidelines, Jason would have to shoulder even more of the burden.

Jason split the practice time at quarterback with Wade for the rest of the week, proving that he could generate the offense but also making some major errors—getting sacked for big losses, fumbling some snaps and handoffs, having passes intercepted. Wade was steady but unspectacular.

Coach Podesta gathered the team after a light workout on Friday.

"Big game tomorrow night," he said. Everyone knew that.

Coach wasted no time making the announcement they'd been anticipating. "Wade will start at quarterback," he said. "He's got the experience and deserves the chance."

Several players voiced agreement, especially the eighth-graders. Jason glanced over at Wade, who nodded his head slowly at the news, a small but triumphant smile on his lips. Jason was slightly relieved. He was much more comfortable at wingback.

"We'll be looking to control the ball," Coach said. "I hope we can get our running game going and not have to rely too much on passing."

He paused and looked directly at Wade. "You've got the whole team behind you, Wade, and you'll have every chance to lead them. But if things aren't going well out there, we'll reevaluate. We've all seen this week that Fiorelli can make big things happen at QB."

"Yeah—good *and* bad," Wade said. "Don't worry, Coach. I'm more than ready for this. . . . I should have been in there all season."

Coach let the remark slide. "Be at the field by five thirty tomorrow, guys," he said. "The game's at seven."

Anthony ran a finger over the old Little League team photo taped to the wall of the Fiorellis' basement. He stopped when he found himself, kneeling next to Jason. "Man, I was a fat little kid, wasn't I?" he said.

"You were a fat *big* kid last time I looked," Miguel remarked from the plaid couch shoved in the corner.

Anthony smirked and grabbed his waist. There was still a small roll there, but he had become a strong, solid athlete in the past year.

"Did you see that look on Wade's face when Coach said he'd be starting?" Anthony asked, dropping onto the couch between Miguel and Lamont.

It had become a ritual for many of the seventh-grade players to gather at the Fiorellis' the night before a game. The basement was small, but there was a TV and some furniture to lounge on. Jason had tacked up posters of rock musicians and some unframed team pictures of the various YMCA and Little League squads he'd played for.

He and his dad had painted the cinder-block foundation walls white that summer, and they'd put a coat of gray on the cement floor. The wet paint had stunk so much that they'd had to spend the night at Mrs. Fiorelli's parents' house in Jersey City.

"Wade," Lamont said with a touch of disgust. "I wanted to smack him." He took off his glasses and wiped them on his button-down shirt. "What's the word for it? Not conceited. *Smug.* He had that smug look, like 'I *told* you all I was better than Fiorelli.'"

"He's not starting because Coach thinks he's better," Anthony said. "Coach is just hoping we can squeak by for one game until Jason gets some more practice. Wade is what they call the *stop-gap* measure."

"I think Vinnie could play better *left*-handed than Wade," Willie Shaw piped in. "Too bad they won't let him do that."

"Where is Vinnie anyway?" Lamont asked. "Thought he was coming by."

"His wrist hurts too much," Jason said. "Sitting in school all day is all he can manage right now."

Vinnie had been over to watch practice a couple of times that week, but left early. He had assured Jason that he'd be at the game, and Coach said he could wear his jersey and stand on the sideline, with the team.

"It's almost like I want Wade to have a bad game just to show how much better Vinnie is," Jason said. "Like throw three interceptions or something."

"We'd lose, man," said Lamont.

"I know. Guess that would be even worse."

Lamont picked up a small rubber basketball and began to dribble. The ceiling was only seven feet high down here, but years before, Jason had rigged up a basketball hoop on the far wall, about a foot below the ceiling. He'd spent hundreds of hours down here, playing alone, inventing opponents and teammates. Often his friends would be over for wild two-on-two games that lasted for hours. Jason's parents didn't mind; there wasn't anything down there to break.

"I don't *want* Wade to do bad; I'm just afraid that he will," Lamont said. "He can throw the ball, but he freezes up and panics whenever the rush is on. The thing I don't like is that he acts like he's so good."

Lamont tossed the ball to Jason, then started jogging toward the basket. "I'm open!" he called.

Jason fired the ball to him and Lamont hauled it in, gently dunking it. "Whoa!" he said. "Nicked my 'fro on the ceiling." He rubbed his head. "I think this room shrunk since the last time we played."

"Yeah," Jason said, smiling. "We need bigger arenas now. Out in the spotlight, in the stadium."

5

A Scared Rabbit

Jason inhaled the crisp October air and glanced over at the bleachers. The Hudson City stadium was packed with spectators, and someone was beating out a steady rhythm on a drum. The crowds had grown each week as the Hornets extended their winning streak. Tonight's game was huge.

Jason watched from the sideline as Lamont teed up the ball for the opening kickoff. Lamont had been chosen as the new placekicker, but in practice his kickoffs had been at least ten yards shorter than Vinnie's. And he barely made half of his extra-point attempts. Hudson City would be running two-point conversion tries in most circumstances.

"Our night!" Jason shouted, rubbing his hands together and jogging a few steps in place. The Bayonne players were stretched across the opposite sideline, looking big and tough in their white uniforms with maroon trim.

Behind the Hudson City bench, Wade was tossing a football back and forth with David Choi. Wade had been his usual arrogant self during warm-up drills, but his passes were on target. Jason had to admit that Wade had a decent arm; it was just that his inflated ego was so fragile. The self-confidence quickly disappeared when the heat was on. Any pressure from the defense forced him into bad throws and bad decisions.

Lamont booted the ball with all his might. The Hudson City players raced down the field as the Bayonne return man waited for the end-over-end kick to come down. He bobbled it but hung on, racing up the center of the field and making a sharp cut behind a blocker. Miguel stopped him cold with a hard tackle.

Assistant Coach Hector Melena tapped on Jason's helmet and said, "Quick meeting of the offense."

Some of the offensive players—Anthony, Sergio, Miguel, and Anderson—also started on defense, but the remaining starters gathered by the bench with Coach Melena. "Patience and power—that's the plan," he said. "We need to establish the run. Jared and Miguel right up the center; Jason on an occasional reverse."

Coach reached over and gripped Wade's jersey and gave him a hard look. "You've got a lot of options here—the running game, the short pass, the fly pattern to Jason. Don't panic and don't run unless you absolutely have to."

"I *know*," Wade said with a scowl. He shot a glare at Jason. Jason just stared back.

"Return team!" Coach Melena said loudly, looking up at the field. "It's fourth down. Bayonne's bringing in the punter."

Jason checked his chinstrap and took a deep breath as he ran onto the field to receive the kick.

Bayonne hadn't advanced far, so Jason lined up at Hudson City's forty-five. The Hornets would have good field position. *Gotta break one,* Jason thought. *All the way to the end zone.*

The kick was short and was drifting toward the far sideline. Jason caught it on the run, reaching full speed within a stride. He dodged past one tackler and was hit by another, but his momentum carried him forward a few more yards, dragging the grunting tackler with him. It was Hudson City's ball inside the Bayonne forty.

Rolling to his feet, Jason had that feeling of controlled excitement that always came with his first touch of the game. He wanted the ball in his hands.

Wade called for a running play: fullback Jared Owen right up the middle. Jason split wide to the left as a decoy. Shoulder pads crashed and helmets collided. The play went nowhere.

"Quarterback draw," Wade said in the huddle.

Jason let out his breath in a huff. Why would

Wade call his own number on the second play from scrimmage?

Wade looked up. "On three. Let's go."

The play did catch the Bayonne defense off guard, and Wade shuffled forward for a three-yard gain.

Third and seven. Wade called for a quick pass to Lamont over the middle, with Jason as the second option. But the Bayonne rush was heavy, and Wade scrambled out of the pocket. The chance to pass to Lamont evaporated in a hurry, but Jason had found a seam and was streaking toward the center of the field, a step ahead of the cornerback.

It didn't matter. Wade got sacked for a six-yard loss. Jason smacked his hand against his thigh in frustration. At fourth and thirteen, the Hornets had little choice but to punt.

"You guys have to *block*!" Wade scolded as the offensive players trotted off the field.

"*You* have to hang in there," Lamont shot back. "You had time to pass. You can't be afraid to take a hit."

"You weren't open," Wade said, a little softer.

"Fiorelli was. That was a touchdown if you hadn't panicked."

Wade just walked away as they reached the sideline, heading for the cooler of Gatorade on the bench.

Jason stood next to Vinnie, who'd been quiet all evening. He was wearing his jersey, but had a windbreaker over it with the cast tucked inside. The right sleeve hung empty. He gave Jason a tight smile. "Nice runback."

Jason shrugged. "Yeah. A wasted opportunity."

Hudson City wasted another one in the second quarter. Anthony made a jarring sack that forced the Bayonne quarterback to fumble, and Miguel scooped up the loose ball and ran it all the way down to the Bayonne seventeen. But a couple of incomplete passes and a two-yard run by Jared left the Hornets with fourth-and-long as the clock reached the two-minute mark. The game was still scoreless.

If Vinnie had been ready, Hudson City might have tried for a field goal. There was no choice but to pass this time.

Jason reached up and grabbed Wade's face mask in the huddle. Not a single pass had come his way. "I'll be open. In the end zone. Get me the ball."

Wade shook loose from Jason's grip and shoved him away. He had sharp words for the linemen. "They've been getting through you guys like cardboard all day," Wade said. "*Hold the line*. Give me a chance to pass the ball without having half their team in my face."

Jason split wide to the left. At the snap he darted forward, gave a hard step toward the sideline, then cut full-speed toward the end zone, freezing the cornerback for a split second. He felt a surge of excitement as he saw nothing but a clear field ahead of him.

Bayonne had dropped a linebacker into the secondary in anticipation of a pass, and the Hudson City line was finally giving Wade the protection he needed. So even though Jason was a step and a half ahead of his defender, Wade couldn't resist the giant hole in front of him. He tucked the ball against his body and barreled straight ahead.

Jason saw the play unfolding and turned quickly, blocking the cornerback who'd been chasing him. Wade had been tackled by a pile of defenders, but he was inside the ten, close to a first down.

The referee blew his whistle sharply, calling a timeout and waving for the yardage markers to be brought onto the field. The players gathered closely to watch the measurement.

A groan came from the Hudson City bleachers, and the Bayonne players leaped and hollered. Wade had landed inches short. The ball went over to Bayonne.

"Would have been a touchdown if you'd thrown the stupid ball!" Jason barked at Wade.

Wade did not respond.

The half ended in a scoreless tie.

In the locker room, Coach Podesta had mostly praise for his players. "The defense has been great," he said. "You've given us two big opportunities. So far we've dominated; we just haven't been able to score."

Coach took a deep breath and let it out in a huff. "Games like this one tend to be decided by one or two big plays. Our big-play guy barely touched the ball in the first half. So Jason, you'll be going in at quarterback."

Jason swallowed hard, but he wasn't really nervous. Without turning his head he shifted his eyes toward Wade, who was scowling slightly but didn't say a word.

Coach had Miguel return the second-half kick-off so Jason could stay on the sideline and take a few extra snaps from Sergio.

"Don't be afraid to try the fly pattern to Calvin," Vinnie said. "Calvin's got that track speed. He ought to be able to break one."

"I'll look for him," Jason said, taking a snap.

Sergio stood and smacked Jason's shoulder pad. "Their defensive line is big and quick, my man, like grizzly bears or something. Don't expect to have all day back there to pass."

"I know. I seen 'em."

Sergio leaned closer. "Wade was too scared to

hang in there. So move if you have to. At least a scared rabbit can get away. Not like that scared giraffe."

Miguel made a good return, and the Hornets set up shop at their own thirty-seven. Jared gained two yards on first down and Miguel got three more on second.

"Wingback pitch," Jason said, calling for his favorite running play. He had scored on that play a couple of games ago, but this time he'd be getting the ball to Calvin.

At the snap, Calvin ran parallel to the line toward Jason, who flipped him the ball and led the way forward. Jason made a nice block on a linebacker, and Calvin slipped ahead for a first down.

"We're moving the ball!" Anthony said with passion as the players huddled around Jason.

"Keep opening those holes," Jason said. "Right down that field."

A couple of running plays moved the ball forward a few yards, but at third down and seven to go, Jason knew it was time to pass.

"Nothing fancy," he said in the huddle. "I'll be looking for Lamont on a slant over the middle or Calvin in the flat. On two. Let's go."

A Bayonne lineman burst into the backfield and Jason was forced to roll out, racing toward the sideline and searching for an open receiver. He didn't see any. And here came another defender, bearing down in a hurry. Jason had to get rid of the ball or take a deep sack.

Calvin was tightly covered, but he was Jason's only option. If he could sling it far enough, maybe Calvin would chase it down.

Jason stopped short, heaved the ball as far as he could, and was immediately tackled hard. He hit the ground with a thud and quickly rolled away from the tackler.

Getting to his knees, Jason was momentarily confused. Players from both teams were running back toward him. And a Bayonne player had the ball!

Jason leaped to his feet and joined the pursuit, but the player was too far ahead. Obviously the pass had been intercepted. And the Bayonne player was on his way to the end zone. He wouldn't be caught.

Jason sprinted after him but never got closer than five yards away.

"Should have taken the sack," Coach said as Jason stepped glumly to the sideline. He put his arm around Jason's shoulder. "Rookie mistake. Let's get back to it. We're still in the game."

Jason looked nervously at the clock as Bayonne grinded out a lengthy drive late in the fourth quarter. "Gotta get the ball back," he said to Vinnie. "I just need one more chance."

The score was still 6–0, but Bayonne was eating up a lot of time. Jason knew that he could pull this one out if the defense could keep the deficit down to one score.

"Stay calm," Vinnie said. "It'll happen; I can feel it in my bones."

Finally, on fourth-and-one at the Hudson City seventeen, Anthony plugged a hole and stopped the Bayonne tailback for a loss. The Hudson City players shouted. The momentum suddenly seemed to be theirs.

Jason raced onto the field and gathered the offensive players around him. "Long way to go," he said. "Just like last week: a couple of big plays and we'll stay undefeated."

The Hornets had two timeouts left and a little less than two minutes to work with. But they also had eighty-two yards to go.

Jason called a play that targeted Calvin as the receiver fifteen yards upfield near the sideline. "Preserve the clock," he said. "Get out of bounds if you can."

He took the snap and stepped back into the pocket, but the defenders were already closing in. Anthony and Sergio and the others were battling to give Jason protection, but white-uniformed arms were reaching high to thwart any passes and the Hornets were being driven backwards.

Jason darted to his left and managed to escape from the horde, but a linebacker brought him down after a three-yard gain. More importantly, the clock was still running.

Jason scrambled to his feet and motioned for his team to line up. He grabbed Calvin's arm and said, "Same play." He hoped the rest of the players would assume that.

The rush this time was even more intense, and a blitzing linebacker was zeroing in from Jason's left. He took off at a sprint to his right, away from Calvin's side of the field, and frantically stayed a stride ahead of the linebacker.

There was Lamont, running parallel to Jason about twenty yards upfield. Jason threw the ball on the run but got little power behind it. It fell to the turf a few yards shy of the receiver.

The incomplete pass stopped the clock, but now it was third and seven. The team huddled up. "Let's not panic," Jason said, as much for himself as for his teammates.

"I was open," Calvin said.

"Couldn't even see you," Jason replied.

"I know. I mean, that play can work again."

"We ran it twice in a row already. Split to the other side." Jason looked up, scanning the defensive alignment. "Lamont—sorry that pass was so lame. Run the same pattern. Let's go!"

The Hornets' line held fast this time, and Jason stayed in the pocket. Calvin was a step ahead of the cornerback and Lamont was also clear. Either option would work. Jason took a step forward and prepared to launch the ball.

A massive, unexpected hit forced all the air from Jason's lungs and sent him sprawling to the ground. Things went black for a fraction of a second as the ball rolled backwards. Jason struggled to get up but the linebacker had him pinned. Players were running past him like a stampede of cattle.

When Jason got to his feet, a Bayonne lineman was in the end zone, holding the ball aloft with one hand as his teammates celebrated around him. The fumble had been scooped up and returned for a touchdown. The Hudson City winning streak was over.

6

Mandatory Pizza

Jason had a rough night, tossing and turning and punching his pillow a couple of times. The coaches and his teammates—most of them, anyway—had insisted that he shouldn't feel responsible for the loss. But there was no disputing those two costly turnovers. He spent several hours just staring at the ceiling of his bedroom. It was well after three A.M. when he finally nodded off.

In his dreams, he was chasing a football around a muddy field, feeling it slip through his fingers every time he thought he had a grip on it. The ball sprouted short, chubby legs and started squealing like a pig, staying just out of Jason's reach as he chased it round and round. Spectators in the bleachers were laughing loudly and hooting at him. Every few seconds, a giant linebacker would knock him flat.

He woke with a start and looked around the room. The sun was just coming up. He put on a sweatshirt and went downstairs. His parents weren't awake yet.

The Sunday newspaper was on the stoop, and Jason carried it in. He scanned the results of the high-school games—Hudson City had lost to Memorial—and read the preview of that afternoon's Giants-Eagles NFL game. Then he turned to the youth sports section.

Dad came down after a few minutes and put his hand on Jason's shoulder. "You all right?" he asked.

"Yeah. I'm embarrassed mostly."

"Don't be."

"Hard not to be."

"You're still in first place."

"Just barely."

	W	L	T	Pct.
Hudson City	5	1	0	.833
Bayonne	4	1	1	.800
Hoboken	4	1	1	.800
West Newark	3	2	1	.600
Liberty	4	3	0	.571
Arlington	2	3	1	.400
South Bergen	2	5	0	.285
Greenville	1	5	0	.167
Palisades	1	5	0	.167

Saturday's scores:

Hoboken 36, Liberty 6

Arlington 21, South Bergen 20

Bayonne 13, Hudson City 0

West Newark 19, Greenville 16

Next week:

Hudson City at Palisades

Arlington at West Newark

Hoboken at Bayonne

Liberty at Greenville

"If you win the next two, you're the champs," Dad said. "It's as simple as that."

"Yeah. As simple as beating Hoboken."

Dad gave a slight laugh. "It's possible. Believe me, you'll bounce back. That was your first time at quarterback in a real game."

"And probably the last."

"You never know," Dad said. "You made some mistakes. That doesn't mean you'll make them again."

Jason rolled his eyes. Those mistakes had been so big that they seemed to overshadow every success he'd ever had in sports.

"It was just two plays, buddy," Dad said. "Two little plays."

"Two *huge* plays," Jason replied. "Two plays that might cost us the entire season."

Anthony phoned in the early afternoon. Jason had been staring at the TV, not really watching the Giants game, just thinking about his failures at quarterback.

"Bro, you okay?" Anthony asked.

"I guess."

"You guess? What's not to be okay about?"

Jason sighed. "Like you don't know?"

"Get over it. Meet us downtown in fifteen minutes."

"What for?"

"We're going for pizza," Anthony said.

"I'm not hungry."

"Sure you are."

"I don't know. . . ."

"I'm telling you," Anthony said. "Villa Roma. No excuses."

"I'll think about it."

"We'll come over and get you if you don't show up. It's mandatory."

"Says who?"

"Me."

"Wow. I guess that's final, huh?"

"You bet it's final. Fifteen minutes."

Twenty-five minutes later Jason was walking on the Boulevard toward the pizza place. The street was busy, but he could see Anthony, Miguel, and Calvin walking toward him. Anthony grinned when he caught sight of Jason.

"We were on our way to drag your butt down here!" Anthony shouted from half a block away.

Jason smiled. He stuck his hands in the pocket of his sweatshirt. "No need. I'm coming."

"You still blaming yourself?" Miguel asked as they met.

Jason shrugged.

"Good," Miguel said. He grinned broadly and grabbed Jason's shoulder. "You blew it, my man. Sure can't blame anybody *else.* Can't blame the line that didn't protect you, or the running backs that couldn't gain any yardage, or the receivers that couldn't get open."

"Or the *starting* quarterback who never got you the ball," Calvin added.

Jason nodded. "Yeah," he said, "I know—T-E-A-M. But it's *mostly* my fault. You all know that."

"Are you the reason we won our first five games?" Anthony asked.

Jason bit down on his lip and squirmed a little. "No. I'm *one* of the reasons."

"But you're the reason we lost last night?"

"The biggest reason."

"The guy who was in your face when you threw the interception was my responsibility," Anthony said. "He knocked me on my butt and took off after you."

"And the guy who caused that fumble blew right by me," Miguel said.

"Okay. You made your point," Jason said. "We all stunk last night."

"Not entirely," Calvin said. "The game was dead even except for two plays."

Jason laughed. "Okay. So now we're back where we started. Two plays—big-time mistakes by the emergency quarterback."

"And now it's over," Anthony said. He was laughing, too. "I'll sit on anybody who brings it up again. Take it out on Palisades next week. Now, I'm starving. Let's go eat."

They spent an hour at Villa Roma, splitting two pizzas and playing pinball and video games. Jason was in a better mood until Wade walked in. He was wearing a leather jacket and a Yankees cap.

Wade was alone. He walked over and leaned against the pinball machine. "Great game last night," he said sarcastically to Jason.

"Oh, hi, Wade," Jason said. He waved at the air. "Hi, all of Wade's friends."

"Real funny," Wade said. "At least I *have* friends."

"And I don't?"

Wade looked around at the group. "Friends of my own kind, I mean."

Jason shook his head and took a step closer to Wade. "You're such an idiot."

Anthony stepped forward, too. "What you sayin', Wade?"

Wade put up a hand, motioning for Anthony to stop. "This doesn't involve you."

"Oh no?" Anthony said. "What's with that crack about his 'own kind'?"

"You know what he meant," Jason said. He kept his eyes squarely on Wade. "I got plenty of white friends, stupid. But you look at these guys and see a bunch of blacks and Mexicans, right? Well I got news for you: They're *all* my kind."

Jason pointed at Anthony. "Lineman, sprinter, shot-putter." He thrust his thumb toward Miguel—"Centerfielder, linebacker"—then toward Calvin—"Soccer player, track guy. My kind of people. And they're all *winners*, Wade, not *whiners*."

"They sure weren't winners last night."

"More than you were."

Wade gave a dismissive laugh. "Oh yeah? I didn't piss the ball away for two Bayonne touchdowns."

"At least I was in there."

"You never should have been."

"I wouldn't have been if you were any good," Jason said. "You were so pathetic the coach had to pull you."

"I bet he's kicking himself now for putting *you* in there. Bet he learned his lesson."

Anthony stepped between Jason and Wade and put a finger on Wade's chest. "You're gonna get us kicked out of here if you don't shut up," he said. "And one of us is going to stomp you if that happens."

"Sure," Wade said. "I'd like to see you try."

"I don't think you would," Anthony said. "It wouldn't be pretty."

"I'm shaking," Wade said sarcastically, but then he softened his tone. "Listen, I didn't mean nothing about 'his own kind.' I got no problem with the rest of you guys." But he glared at Jason again. "Don't hold your breath waiting for the ball to come your way next week. I'll be looking for a receiver who doesn't fumble."

Wade turned to leave the restaurant. Miguel balled up a napkin and threw it at him. It hit him in the back and fell to the floor.

"Biggest jerk I ever met," Calvin said. "How did he get to be a *quarterback*?"

7
Halloween

Coach Podesta blew his whistle midway through Monday's practice session and gathered the team around him. He hadn't said a word so far about Saturday's loss, just put the team through the usual routine of calisthenics, stretching, tackling drills, and passing. They'd been scrimmaging for about fifteen uninspired minutes, with Wade at quarterback and Jason at wingback.

"I'm not seeing much life out there today," Coach said. "You're either dwelling too much on that loss to Bayonne or planning your Halloween costumes."

Many of the players laughed. Halloween was two days away, and Coach had said he'd end practice early on Wednesday so the players could watch the city's parade that evening.

"Let's refocus, all right?" Coach said. "Palisades always gives us a tough game, so we'll need everything we've got. Do we have enough?"

"Yes!" shouted some of the players.

"You sure?"

"Yes!" yelled everybody else.

"Okay. Back to the scrimmage. Fiorelli at quarterback. Let's go."

"Wait!" Wade shouted as the players ran back to their positions. "You kidding me, Coach? You still haven't given up on that loser?"

Coach stared at Wade for several seconds. Wade turned red and looked away. "Sorry," he said softly.

"Take a seat, Wade," Coach said. "We win and lose as a team. And I make the calls around here."

Coach walked over to the huddle and faced Jason. "The starting job is yours," he said firmly. "Run the team."

Jason nodded and called for a handoff to Miguel. "I guess I'm the quarterback," he said. "You guys with me?"

"Always have been," Calvin said.

"Then let's do it. On one."

Jason hurried through dinner on Wednesday and dashed toward the Boulevard. The parade was scheduled to begin in less than an hour, but he and some others needed to prepare their costumes. It was dark as he walked excitedly along 12th Street. A breeze was blowing, but the night wasn't too cold.

Vinnie was waiting as planned beneath the digital clock outside the bank. The clock said 6:13 and forty-two degrees.

It had been a good practice that day. Jason had found Calvin for a long touchdown pass, and later he'd dashed thirty yards for one of his own.

"You're the man now," Vinnie said as they shook left hands. "No question about that."

"For two games only," Jason said. "It's your job again next season, believe me."

"Hope so," Vinnie said.

"I know so. DiMarco-to-Fiorelli for years to come. State champions by the time we finish high school."

"That'd be something."

"Look at this town," Jason said, waving his arm up the Boulevard, which was packed with small stores and restaurants—the block they were on included Lupita Music, which had sponsored his first Little League team, and the Envigado Bakery, which provided doughnuts and juice for many of the Saturday-morning YMCA leagues.

He'd always felt supported here, in this little town in the shadow of the giant New York City and the bigger neighbors of Hoboken and Jersey City. He loved the Hudson City YMCA, where he'd become hooked on athletics during a season of indoor floor hockey as a first-grader. He'd won his first championship as a second-grader in that gym, leading the purple-T-shirted Hudson City National Bank Buckeyes basketball team to victory. So many of the businesses in town kicked in by sponsoring teams and soccer clinics and youth basketball tournaments.

"I love it here," Jason said. "The people are good. They deserve something big. We can make that happen."

Vinnie lifted his cast. "Maybe you can. I'm damaged goods."

"You'll heal. I'm talking later—other years. This group we've got can be big-time champions. We just have to stick together and *work* it."

"I'm with you."

"And I'm with you. The future starts now. It starts Saturday. We'll beat Palisades, then turn it all toward Hoboken. After that, who knows? We'll just keep getting better . . . until we're great."

They'd walked a couple of blocks and turned down 14th toward Anthony's. "Time to paint the faces," Vinnie said.

"Yeah. I decided to be orange," Jason said. The group was going to wear their football jerseys and paint their faces wild colors. They weren't in the parade, but lots of spectators dressed up for the event.

"We should go through the cemetery later," Jason said.

"What for?"

"It's spooky. And it's Halloween, man. If there's ever going to be ghosts around, it'd be tonight."

Vinnie shrugged. The cemetery was very small, only about a square block, and was surrounded by a tall fence of thin iron posts. It overlooked the cliffs on the edge of town, which overlooked the Hudson River and New York City.

"I don't think anybody's been buried in there for eighty years," Vinnie said.

"So? Ghosts stay around forever."

Vinnie laughed. "No such thing."

"How do you know?"

Vinnie shrugged again. "I guess I don't."

"It's Halloween, buddy. Strange things happen."

Anthony's mother had bought several tubes of face paint, but she insisted the kids put it on in the basement. "That stuff's greasy and it smells," she said. "Don't wipe it on my walls."

Anthony had a big glob of yellow paint in his palm. "I'm doing a yellow face and a red nose," he said. "We got trick-or-treat candy, Ma?"

"We got plenty. But save that for the little kids who come around. You can get your own."

Within a few minutes, Jason had an orange face, Vinnie was green, Calvin was blue, and Lamont had green and yellow stripes.

"Let's go get a spot," Anthony said. "I don't want to be behind a bunch of people."

They walked up and stood at the curb by the post office, about midway along the parade route. They could hear the high-school band in the distance, warming up.

"Be sure to make a lot of noise for my brother," Lamont said.

"What's he do?"

"Cymbals. He has to walk backwards because he's in charge of the percussionists."

"He walks backwards and plays the cymbals at the same time?" Anthony asked.

"Yup."

Anthony shook his head slowly. "He must be a musical genius. How come you didn't get none of that?"

"I did," Lamont said. "You never heard me sing?"

"Not what I'd call singing."

"You don't know talent when you hear it."

The parade had started with a line of Boy Scouts carrying a Troop 47 banner, then a fire engine. The boys whooped and waved when the Hornets' junior cheerleading squad went by. That was followed by a couple of police officers on horseback, then some young girls twirling batons, and then the high-school band.

"Go Omar!" Lamont shouted as his brother went past. Omar looked over and winked, then banged his cymbals together. The band was playing The Doors' song "Light My Fire." Omar was writhing in rhythm with the song.

"Good band," Anthony said.

"Better than the football team," Lamont replied. "This year, anyway."

Members of the city council and the mayor went by on a float, tossing candy to the crowd. Jason picked up a mini chocolate bar that landed by his feet and unwrapped it. He popped the whole thing into his mouth.

The next group surprised them, not because it

was a troop of Brownies, but because Wade was walking alongside them. He was holding hands with a tiny girl who looked a lot like him. The girl had trouble walking but was gamely marching on.

"Did you join the Girl Scouts, Wade?" shouted Lamont.

Wade gave an embarrassed grin. "My sister's got a leg problem," he said. "But she's toughing it out."

"You earning a merit badge for helping her?" Calvin asked.

Wade rolled his eyes. "Real funny."

Wade's sister waved to the boys. She said something to Wade that Jason couldn't hear, but he patted her head and smiled at her. They kept walking. Jason turned and watched them go. It was something to see Wade thinking outside of himself, helping his little sister like that.

The parade only lasted about thirty minutes, trailed by hundreds of younger kids in costume. A party was to follow at the Y, and prizes would be given for the best attire. Jason had won third place once when he dressed up as a Ghostbuster.

But they were kind of old for that now.

They walked up and down the Boulevard a couple of times, getting free candy at some of the shops. Jason almost suggested that they walk up to the cemetery, but decided that he didn't want a big rowdy group for that. So he hung out for an hour or so until most of the group had gone home. Only Vinnie and Anthony remained.

"Ready?"

Vinnie looked at his cast and frowned. "I don't know if I can get over the fence," he said.

"We can squeeze in through the gate," Jason said. "I've done it."

"Done what?" Anthony asked.

"Snuck into the cemetery. Sound okay?"

"Okay by me," Anthony said. "The way we look, any goblins in there tonight will think we fit right in."

Hudson City is small, densely populated, and busy with foot traffic and automobiles. Many of the houses don't even have yards, and the ones that do exist are small. It's hard to find any place that isn't at least partly lit by a streetlight. But if you walk up past St. Joseph's Church and make your way over to Terrace Street, then past the high-school baseball field and head for the cliffs, you reach the darkest stretch of town.

The boys walked past rows of tightly clustered homes decorated with pumpkins—large blown-up plastic ones that sat on lawns, and carved real ones on porches with jack-o'-lantern faces lit by candles.

On one side of Terrace, at the corner of Washington, is a small city park—just a bunch of tall maple trees, some wooden benches, a swing set, and a blacktop basketball court. If you follow the path to the edge of the park, you reach the gate to the tiny cemetery, where some of the city's founders are buried and a few Civil War soldiers. Nobody goes down there much. The plots were all filled by the first half of the previous century, so not too many city residents have relatives buried there that they'd remember knowing.

There was a chain around one old post and through the first post of the gate, but there was some slack in it. Jason and Vinnie had no trouble slipping in, and Anthony sucked in his breath and managed to squeeze through, too.

The brush was dense near the gate. And though the leaves on the trees had turned brown, many had not yet fallen. Very little moonlight got through to the ground.

"Could use a flashlight," Anthony whispered. A misty condensation followed his words. The evening had turned cold.

"Just go slow," Jason replied.

They walked carefully, each step bringing with it the smell of dying grass and of the few dry, brittle leaves that had reached the ground.

As their eyes adjusted to the darkness, Jason stopped in front of a small slate gravestone. JACOB ADDISON. JAN 15 1836–NOV 11 1904.

"The guy's been dead for more than a century," Jason whispered.

"That's nothing," Anthony said. "Here's one from eighteen thirty-one."

They looked around some more, finding dozens of graves from the early 1800s, including many children who'd died soon after birth.

"A lot of kids never even got to grow up back then," Vinnie said.

The narrow dirt path circled the perimeter of the grounds. It had been built long before automobiles, so the lane was tight. The trees were tall and old, and the gravestones were cracked and covered with lichens.

Jason stopped and stared at a marker from 1827, topped by a marble lamb and the simple words *At Rest*. He was thinking hard about these people's life spans. *1807–1861. 1840–1842. 1833–1918*. Some lives had been long, some very short. And all had ended a long time ago.

They stood quietly, respectfully for a few minutes, glancing at the gravestones, at the moon above the trees, at the skyline of New York City visible on the other side of the Hudson.

"Life matters," Jason said finally. "You have to leave a mark."

"You have to do what you can do," Anthony replied. "Win or lose, you have to go after it."

Jason turned to Anthony, thinking of something equally solemn to add. But he'd forgotten that they were still wearing face paint. The sight of Anthony's yellow face and red nose made him laugh instead.

"What?" said Anthony.

Jason pointed to his own orange face.

Anthony smiled. "Let's get back to town," he said.

They started walking, then stopped and looked back across the cemetery. "I never thought about it before tonight," Jason said, "but life is short. We gotta make every day count for something, don't we?"

8

A Secret Play

Palisades kept things interesting for half a game, going into the locker room with an 8–6 lead. But the Hudson City defense clamped down in the second half, Jason sprinted fifty-one yards for a touchdown on a quarterback keeper, and Miguel bulled through for a fourteen-yard scoring run and then added the two-point conversion. Final score: Hudson City 20, Palisades 8.

The announcement that Hoboken had scored a narrow win over Bayonne that same evening left a simple scenario. Whoever won the Hudson City vs. Hoboken game on the final Saturday would walk away with the EJJFL title.

"It'll be like a bowl game!" Anthony said as the Hornets got off the bus after the ride home from Palisades.

Jason raised his fist and shook it. "Like the Super Bowl. Winner take all."

"Hoboken has a dynasty going," Miguel said. "They seem to win the league every year."

"Time to end it," Jason added. "Dynasties are made to be broken."

"Overthrown, you mean," Anthony said.

"Whatever."

Wade slipped past them in a hurry. He hadn't played at all, barely moving from the bench, where he'd sat with his helmet on. He hadn't budged when the Hornets had scored, and had nothing to say when the game ended in victory.

Jason started to say something. A simple, sarcastic "Nice game, Wade" would have been enough, but he caught himself and stayed quiet. Why stoop to that level?

Miguel smacked Jason on the back. "Your buddy there must have splinters in his butt from all that bench time," he said with a laugh.

Jason shrugged. "Yeah, well, he earned them. Too much mouth on him."

"He's history, man. You proved that tonight."

Jason nodded slowly. As much as he disliked Wade, he couldn't help feeling sorry for him, too. Sitting on the bench for an entire game must be agonizing. Especially knowing that you'd blown a huge opportunity to be the starter.

Tuesday afternoon Jason sat waiting for the bell to ring, ending the social studies class. The teacher had just handed back the tests from the day before. Jason had not done well.

"Let's see," said Anthony, reaching across the aisle for Jason's paper. "A C-minus? When was the last time you got less than a B on anything?"

Jason rolled his eyes. "Been a while," he said.

"Didn't you study?"

Jason turned in his seat to face his friend. "I thought I did." He took the paper back and stared at it. "Guess nothing sunk in. Everything I try to think about turns into one subject this week: Hoboken."

Anthony shook his head. He showed Jason his own paper, which was marked with an A. "We'll beat Hoboken, Jason. Stop worrying."

"They beat Bayonne last week," Jason said. "Bayonne clobbered us."

"Bayonne did *not* clobber us, Fiorelli. Get over that. Like my ma always tells me when I think I can't accomplish something, 'Dis*avow* yourself of that notion.'"

Jason smiled. "Wish we could just play the game tonight and be done with it. I can't wait four more days."

"You can wait. You better wait. The game's not till Saturday. And we got another social studies test on Friday."

It was nearly dark as Jason and Wade stood face-to-face on the practice field Thursday, sizing each other up, but listening to Coach Podesta go over the strategy. Jason rubbed the toe of his cleats into the soft dirt and scratched at a tiny zit on his jaw.

The other players had left the field for home after a bruising workout. Coach had kept some key members of the offense behind for a few minutes as he went over a new play, but even they were gone now. Only the two quarterbacks remained—the two biggest rivals on the team.

"Saturday night is going to be brutal," Coach said. "Hoboken is big and strong—like Bayonne, but quicker. It'll be the kind of game where two teams just slug each other around the field, and one big play can mean the difference between a championship and a major disappointment."

Jason looked across the field toward the parking lot, where Anthony and Miguel were talking. He could hear them laughing—they always seemed loose. He was that way, too; at least he had been. These past few weeks had been tough—the shock of losing Vinnie to injury, the fumble and interception against Bayonne, the pressure of becoming the starting QB against Palisades. Now, with the biggest game of his life staring him in the face, Jason was a bundle of nerves. He wanted to be that guy he'd been—joking, making wisecracks, succeeding while having fun.

"I don't know if we'll even get to run this play," Coach was saying, "or need to. But you two have to be ready if we do. It takes two quarterbacks. You need to work *together*."

Wade picked up the football and tossed it from hand to hand. "Just put the ball in my hands," he said. "I know what to do with it."

Coach stuck his hands in his pockets and frowned. "You know what to do with it? Show me. Run the play."

Jason took the ball and mimed the action of lining up behind an invisible center. The crescent moon was up early, shining just above the horizon. Jason pulled back the ball and dropped into passing position, and he and Wade ran the play just as Coach had instructed them to.

"Not bad," Coach said. "Let's do it a few more times."

They stayed at it until it was too dark to continue, successfully making the play more often than not. Of course, there were no defenders on the field.

"It's a great play when it works," Coach said. "Not too complicated, but effective. The key here is you two guys"—he grabbed both of their face masks and held tight—"being in sync. That will make all the difference."

They walked off the field together, and Coach got into his pickup truck and drove off. Anthony and Miguel were gone. Jason and Wade stood alone in the parking lot.

Jason cleared his throat. "Moon's out," he said, stating the obvious.

Wade nodded but looked away. "Supposed to be clear on Saturday. Not too cold."

"I heard."

Wade let out his breath in a long, audible exhalation. He wiped his nose with his sleeve and took a step toward the street. "You staying here all night?" he asked.

"No."

"Let's go then."

They walked up toward the Boulevard, not

talking. Jason felt uneasy; he still didn't like Wade, but he no longer felt as if a fight could break out at any time. Either way, Jason had the upper hand. He was the starter now; Wade had only this one surprise play that might not even get called. But Jason was glad Wade had that. At least he *might* be able to contribute.

The streets were busy. It was that in-between time, with New York City commuters arriving home on buses, lots of cars on the Boulevard, kids hurrying home for dinner, and shoppers picking up bread and milk at the grocery store or takeout pizza or Chinese food. All the streetlights were on and everybody seemed to be on the move.

"You ever win a championship before?" Wade asked.

"A few," Jason replied. They were standing alongside the corner grocery store at Ninth and the Boulevard. "Basketball last year. Some Y leagues."

Wade took his helmet and placed it over a parking meter, so it looked like a very skinny player. That made him smile. He snapped the chin guard to secure it. "I never won anything yet," Wade said. "Four years of Little League, three years of junior football, and two basketball seasons. Never even a second place."

Jason shrugged. "Nobody can do it alone."

"I know. But if Coach gives me another chance on Saturday like he says he might, I'll show 'em."

"It's not about *showing* anybody anything," Jason said. It annoyed him that Wade didn't get it, that winning in team sports like football or basketball demanded team spirit and cooperation. But he felt for him, too. Years of playing with Vinnie and Miguel and the others had taught Jason a lot about teamwork. He couldn't really blame Wade for not having learned those things. But if the opportunity arose on Saturday to use the new play, he didn't want Wade's need for individual attention to mess up the whole thing.

"It's not about showing off or showing up or showing *anything*," Jason said again. "When we put the team first, we all win."

Wade nodded, but he didn't seem convinced. "Easy for you to say." He went into a boxing stance and threw a few punches at his helmet, which was still hanging on the parking meter. "All I know is I shoulda been in there all season. Coach never had enough confidence in me just because we lost a lot last year. That's why he went with Vinnie."

Jason folded his arms and shook his head. "Vinnie's a great quarterback," he said. "We haven't been the same since he got hurt."

"That's 'cause Coach made the wrong choice again. He yanked me after half a game against Bayonne. And I hadn't even done anything wrong."

"Hadn't done much right, either, you gotta admit that."

"Look what happened when he put you in."

"I ain't forgotten," Jason said. "Believe me."

Wade took his helmet off the meter and watched as a police car went by. Its lights were flashing, but the siren was not going. "You thirsty or anything?" he asked, not making eye contact.

"Yeah."

"Come on." Wade led the way into the grocery

store. He took a Coke out of a cooler near the checkout and walked over to pay. Jason got one of his own. For a second he'd thought Wade might be buying, but apparently not. They paid separately and left the store.

"Which way you headed?" Wade asked.

"That way," Jason replied, pointing uptown.

"I'm going the other way. See you later."

"Right." Jason walked away, taking a gulp of soda. *What was that all about?* he wondered. Wade was strange. It was almost as if he wanted to be friendly but didn't quite know how. He always managed to say something stuck-up or selfish.

What would happen if Coach told them to run the new play late in a close game? Would Wade try to prove he was a hero, or would he just perform the task he'd been assigned?

He'd have to wait and see. Maybe they'd be so far ahead that it wouldn't even matter. But that wasn't very likely against Hoboken. The most likely scenario was a tight, tough game that went down to the final seconds.

To himself, Jason seemed to be as different from Wade as two kids could be. But maybe the coach believed differently. He seemed to think that combining their talents might be the best way to win Saturday's game.

9

Who's Invincible?

Warming up on Saturday night, they all seemed to feel it. This notion of Hoboken as a nearly unbeatable force. As if Hudson City's first-place position in the standings—by the slimmest of margins—was all just a sham. That after tonight, Hoboken would retake its rightful place at the top.

Calvin was staring off into the distance as he stretched his legs near the sideline. Lamont kept looking over at the Hoboken players. "Wow, those boys are *large*," he said a couple of times.

Jason stepped away from the backs and

receivers, walking over to Vinnie DiMarco. Vinnie was in uniform tonight, but his wrist was still in a cast and Coach Podesta had said there was no way he would play. He'd let him suit up simply because it was the final game of the season.

"Things seem strange to you?" Jason asked.

"Like what?"

"Everybody seems worried. Or doomed. You feel it?"

Vinnie shrugged and glanced over at the team. "They're quieter than usual, I guess. Probably nervous."

"Or scared stiff."

Hudson City was 6–1, and Hoboken stood at 5–1–1. Everybody knew what was at stake.

"I don't think those guys are scared," Vinnie said, pointing toward Anthony and Sergio and some other linemen, who were doing a blocking drill and banging into each other hard.

"Or him." Vinnie indicated Miguel, running a full-speed sprint near the end zone.

Jason fiddled with his chinstrap and looked up at the bleachers, which were rapidly filling with spectators. "Maybe it's just me," he said.

Vinnie put his hand on Jason's shoulder. "You'll be fine as soon as the game starts," he said. "You're just feeling the pressure."

"Sure wish you were playing quarterback," Jason said. "I'd much rather catch the ball than throw it."

Miguel received the opening kickoff and returned it to the Hudson City thirty-five. Jason trotted onto the field, feeling like he might throw up from nervousness. Hoboken's defensive players were big and furious.

He took a deep breath and called the first play, a simple handoff to Jared between the center and right guard—Sergio and Anthony.

Hoboken had its linebackers packed tight behind the line, ready to exert a lot of pressure. Coach had warned that they were tough to pass against, constantly blitzing.

But Anthony and Sergio bolted forward and opened a hole, and Jared ran through for nearly seven yards. He bounced up quickly and ran back to the huddle.

"Nice blocking," Jason said.

"All night," Anthony said. "We'll own these guys."

Jason called for a quarterback keeper, right through the same hole. He faked a handoff to Miguel and darted for the spot. But this time the hole was plugged by a linebacker. Jason was stopped cold.

Third and three. He called for a short pass play—Calvin in the flat or Lamont over the middle. But he never even got the pass off. As soon as he dropped back, a lineman was all over him. Six-yard loss. Fourth and nine.

But Vinnie was right. The nervousness Jason had felt before the game was gone. He'd been hit hard twice, but nothing bad had happened. These guys were tough, but they weren't invincible.

The Hudson City defense held tight as well, and the Hornets managed a couple of first downs the next time they had the ball. Things were going fine. Hoboken scored on a short drive after a long punt return, but Hudson City was very much in the game.

Late in the second quarter, with a third down and six coming up from the Hornets' forty, Jason was surprised to see Wade running toward the huddle. He grabbed Miguel's arm and said, "I'm in for you." Turning to Jason, he said, "Coach wants us to run the lateral."

Jason kneeled in the huddle and said, "Wade's at tailback. It's a simple lateral to him to the right. Receivers should run the routes they do on play eighty-three, but this is a running play. On two."

At the snap Jason dropped back as if to pass, but turned to his right and pitched the ball to Wade. Wade cut behind Anderson at tackle and ripped into the secondary, gaining eleven yards before being brought down.

Wade leaped up and shook his fist. Hudson City was inside Hoboken territory for the first time all night.

Less than a minute remained before halftime. Jason ran a quarterback sweep for a few yards, then completed a short pass to Lamont. A long pass to Calvin fell incomplete, so it was fourth down with just a few seconds left.

Wade came back onto the field. "The lateral again," he said to Jason.

Jason nodded. He knew this was a setup. Coach wanted Hoboken to expect the lateral anytime Wade came into the backfield. Wade gained about seven yards this time, but the clock ran out as he was tackled.

Halftime score: Hoboken 7, Hudson City 0.

"We may need you after all," Jason said to Vinnie as they jogged toward the locker room.

"How?"

"Low-scoring game like this one, an extra point could be huge. Think you could kick one?"

"I know I could," Vinnie said. "Coach said no way, but maybe . . ."

They stopped running as they reached the path to the lockers. "You know," Jason said, "if we tie these guys, we win the championship. We'd have more wins than they do."

"That's true," Vinnie said. "Win or tie, it's ours. They need a win to get the title."

"We have to get into the end zone first, but that'd be something, huh? A championship-winning extra point from the guy with the broken wrist."

Vinnie shook his head, but he had to smile. "Let's hope it doesn't come down to that. Get us a couple of touchdowns and be done with it."

Both defensive units were outstanding in the second half. Jason ran for a first down and later passed for another, but the Hornets didn't get close to the end zone.

Anthony and Sergio led the Hudson City defense, which kept Hoboken in check. Both teams' punters got a lot of work. The clock showed less than four minutes to go in the fourth quarter as Jason took the field for perhaps the final time, still trailing 7–0.

Anthony punched Jason lightly on the arm. The big lineman was covered with sweat and dirt, and his lips were damp and bloody. "You're the man, Fiorelli," he said. "We've worked too hard not to win this thing. Do something special."

"Help me out then," Jason said. "Quarterback draw. Right behind you."

The Hornets had the ball just short of midfield, but they'd gained very little yardage this half. Jason looked from face to face before breaking the huddle—Anthony, Sergio, and Anderson had been in on nearly every play of the game. They were exhausted. But each of them looked as fired-up as ever.

Jason took the snap, dropped back a step, faked the ball to Miguel, and dodged through the hole behind Anthony. He broke one tackle and surged forward, finally being brought down at the Hoboken forty-six.

"Nice one!" Sergio shouted.

"These guys are tired," Anthony said as they huddled up again. "We can wear them down. Plenty of time. Keep running."

A handoff to Jared went for a first down, and then Miguel broke loose for twelve more yards. They'd reached the thirty. The clock showed 2:47.

Jason felt a new rush of excitement. They were moving the ball. He called his own number again, this time following Anderson ahead for a five-yard gain.

"Yeah!" Jason said in the huddle. "Right in their faces. I'm taking it again. Just drive 'em out of the way."

He was feeling it now; he was taking over this game. He set up behind Sergio, looking over the defense, planning his path through the line.

He called out the signals with new confidence. He'd get another first down, maybe even break free for a score. Here was the ball, into his hands. And there it went, slipping free to the ground.

He'd fumbled the snap. The ball was bouncing away! Jason dove for it, grabbing it with both hands and yanking it toward his chest. Two, three Hoboken linemen were on top of him, but he had it secured.

The play lost three yards. Jason got to his feet and looked over at the sideline. Coach Podesta was signaling for a pass.

"Sorry," Jason said in the huddle before calling the play.

"It's nothing," Anthony said. "Forget it. Just make the throw, Jason. You'll have time."

He had time, but not enough, as none of the receivers got free. Jason scrambled away from the pursuers and raced across the field, but he knew his only options were an incomplete pass or a big loss. He was hit as he threw, but he managed to get the ball away.

So now it was fourth down and eight. Jason got to his feet and saw Wade running onto the field toward him. Wade grabbed Jason's sleeve and gave him a serious look. Then he nodded and said, "Coach says to run it."

Jason swallowed hard and nodded back. The secret play was risky, but if it worked it could pay off in a big way. If it failed, Hoboken would take possession and simply run out the clock.

Jason took a deep breath as the team huddled up. "The patterns are basically the same as play eighty-three," he said. "To the defense it'll look like the lateral we ran at the end of the first half. But we need a little more time; you guys have to block like you never did before. Especially the right side. On three."

Jason caught Wade's eyes as they broke the huddle. The look, which lasted just a fraction of a second, said more than any words they'd spoken. *This is bigger than either one of us. The whole season is riding on this play.*

Wade lined up in the backfield alongside Miguel. Jason inhaled deeply, then called the signals. He felt the grain of the leather as he took the snap from Sergio and dropped quickly back to pass. But then he pivoted and tossed a lateral to Wade, who was running to the right.

Jason darted through the line between Sergio and Anthony, who were fiercely blocking the Hoboken linemen. He was a receiver again! The defensive backs were concentrating on Calvin and Lamont and Miguel, so Jason found a seam, cutting toward the sideline. He was in the clear. Wade's pass was soft but on target, floating in the air at shoulder height. It was Jason's first catch in three weeks. He immediately turned upfield with the ball and reached full speed.

Calvin made a terrific block on the man who was covering him, sending the player sprawling to the turf. The field was wide open. Jason ran like a sprinter, cradling the ball and knowing he wouldn't be caught. It was only a matter of seconds until he raced into the end zone.

Lamont was the first to reach him, throwing both arms around him and lifting him off the ground. Calvin and Miguel were right behind, smacking his helmet and yelling.

But this was no time to celebrate.

"That's only half the battle," Jason said. "We're still a point behind."

Jared had come back onto the field to replace Wade, bringing in the play from the coach. "He says to run the quarterback sneak."

Jason looked to the sideline and caught Coach Podesta's attention. He made a kicking motion, hoping instead that Vinnie might get sent onto the field to try to tie the game, but Coach shook his head. They'd either win the game or lose it on this play.

Jason put his hand on Anthony's shoulder. "Just move 'em back. I'm going right behind you and Sergio. All the power we got now. This is the championship, right here."

He set up behind Sergio and scanned the defense. The Hoboken players were packed in, expecting a run. The linebackers were right behind the line, ready to charge forward on the snap and plug any holes. Sergio and Anthony and the others would have to come up with heroic efforts.

Jason locked eyes with the middle linebacker and saw an intense fury. And that split second of distraction was all that was needed to mess up his handling of the snap. The ball hit the meat of Jason's hand and slid to his thigh. He grabbed at it, bobbled it, and finally hung on, but any chance to force his way through the line had been lost. There was no place to go but back.

Jason looped into the backfield, racing to get away from the onslaught. He angled away from the goal line, back to the ten, then the fifteen, as defenders closed in from every angle. It was chaos, but it was a thing of beauty as Jason dodged past a defensive end, twisted away from a linebacker, and shot past two more pursuers as he ran parallel to the goal line. If he could turn that last corner, he'd score, but the Hoboken safety had the perfect angle to make the tackle.

Jason saw him coming. But he also saw Miguel, alone in the end zone, waving frantically for the ball. Jason left his feet as the safety crashed into him, unloading a wobbly pass that floated toward Miguel and the victory.

Jason went down hard, landing on his back with the defender on top. He heard the triumphant yelling, but which team was it coming from?

And here came his answer—Anthony yanking him to his feet and shouting, "Yes!"

Miguel was leaping in the end zone, and his teammates were swarming around him. Hudson City had the lead!

Jason walked stiffly to the sideline. That tackle had hurt. But now the championship was in their grasp. Just another strong defensive effort. Just a couple of minutes.

Someone gripped his arm as he reached the sideline. He turned and saw Wade's grinning face.

Jason had to smile, too. "Great pass," he said.

"Great run," Wade replied. "We're gonna win this thing."

"Yeah, we are."

They stood next to each other as the kickoff teams took the field, but they didn't have much more to say. They'd both contributed; that was enough. Jason was breathing heavily and sweating, and his heart was pumping like crazy. He stared at the scoreboard again just to make sure. Hudson City 8, Hoboken 7.

When it ended a few moments later—the Hoboken quarterback's long pass soared incomplete—the Hornets ran onto the field in triumph. Jason found Anthony and climbed up his back as Miguel and Calvin and the others swarmed toward them.

Helmets off, arms raised, voices hoarse from

yelling, the Hornets stayed on the field for a long time, hardly believing that they'd won it. Jason finally dropped to his knees, watching as the Hoboken players walked slowly toward their bus. The bleachers were emptying out, but lots of spectators were still there, on their feet, sharing the moment with the Hornets.

"You're some quarterback," Vinnie said, his face a giant smile.

"This is just the beginning," Jason replied. "And *you're* the quarterback. Don't forget that. I was just the emergency guy."

"That sure looked like an emergency on that conversion," Vinnie said. "You must have run about four hundred yards back there, scrambling around. Looked like every guy on the Hoboken team had a shot at you. You were unbelievable."

"Just didn't want to lose," Jason said, getting to his feet. "Didn't want to let these guys down."

Anthony walked over and gave Jason a hug. He was crying as he said, "Beautiful game, huh? Like I said, Fiorelli, you are the man."

"Time for pizza, I think."

"Yeah," Anthony said. He wiped his eyes. "Time for pizza."

They walked off the field. Spectators leaving the parking lot were beeping their horns to celebrate the win.

Jason saw Wade near the sideline, staring over at them. "Come on," Jason said, waving his arm.

"Where to?" Wade asked.

"Villa Roma. Come on, we earned it."

Wade thought for a second, a confused look on his face. Then he broke into a half-smile and said, "Yeah. I can do that. . . . Okay."

So Jason, Anthony, Miguel, Calvin, and Vinnie walked up to the Boulevard, trailed closely by Wade, Sergio, and Lamont. They looked exhausted and muddy and excited and proud.

They looked like a team full of winners.

* * *

Read an excerpt from

SOUTHPAW

Jimmy stepped off the mound and jogged toward the dugout, being careful not to step on the first-base line. That'd be bad luck. He was excited now. He'd done well on this first afternoon of tryouts.

The day was overcast and cool, and a few small patches of snow were still melting in the shady spots near the left-field fence. But the baseball diamond was clear and mostly dry. A trickle of sweat ran from Jimmy's unruly hair onto his cheek. He quickly wiped it away.

The muscular kid that Jimmy had just struck out was frowning as he put his bat in the rack. "What was your name again?" the kid asked.

Jimmy tossed his mitt onto the rickety wooden bench and smiled. Not many kids had bothered talking to him since his arrival in town. "Jimmy Fleming," he said eagerly. "My friends back home call me Flem."

The kid made a sour face and said, "Flem?" He thought for a second, squinting and giving the lanky newcomer a good looking-over. "I don't know where 'back home' is, but to me phlegm is something you hack up and spit out." And he did just that to demonstrate.

"Home is Pennsylvania. And yeah, I've heard all the jokes," Jimmy said, looking away. "They never bothered me."

The other kid shrugged. "I'm Spencer Lewis," he said, not smiling. "But you already knew that."

"I did?"

"You ought to."

Jimmy raised his eyebrows. "That so?"

"Starting shortstop. Leadoff hitter."

"Wow," Jimmy said with a lot of sarcasm. This kid seemed pretty full of himself. Jimmy decided to needle him a bit. "So I struck out a big star, huh?"

Spencer winced but gave a half smile. "I ain't hearing that noise," he said. "Everybody knows the pitchers are ahead of the hitters in March. It might take me a minute to get used to a lefty like you, with that weird delivery, but tomorrow will be different."

The coach had said there'd be a full week of try-outs before he cut the roster to eighteen players. Jimmy had counted twenty-nine out for the squad.

"The team's pretty well set, you know," Spencer said, "especially my boys on the pitching staff."

"I think I got a shot," Jimmy replied. He could see that Spencer was going to keep busting his chops, letting him know he was an outsider.

"You got okay stuff. We might be able to use you some in relief."

Jimmy gave Spencer a mean look. "I guess the coaches'll decide that, won't they?"

Spencer shrugged. "Yeah. But they want guys who are gonna fit in, Flem. People who know the score."

"I been pitching for four years," Jimmy said.

"Yeah, in the sticks."

"Sticks? Where'd you find a word like that? 1920?"

"What do you call it?"

"Home."

"Call it whatever you want," Spencer said. "All I'm saying is there's a big difference between Hudson City and cow country."

That stung a little. There actually had been a dairy farm about two hundred yards from the Flemings' house in Pennsylvania. Jimmy's mother owned a horse that she boarded there.

Jimmy just smiled, went into a batting stance, and gave a gentle swing. "Strike three," he said.

"Like I was saying, I ain't used to lefties right now."

"And like I said, I think I got a shot. Besides, you ever heard of Christy Mathewson?" he asked, referring to the Hall of Fame pitcher who had grown up in northeastern Pennsylvania.

"Yeah. So?"

"Where do you think he's from?"

Spencer laughed. "That was like forever and two days ago, Flem."

Head Coach Wimmer had walked over and cleared his throat. He was old and paunchy and had been leading the Hudson City Middle School seventh-grade team for more than thirty years. "All right, boys," he said, eyeing the bunch. "Pretty good for a first day. You're not quite ready for Yankee Stadium, but we'll whip you into shape.

"Go on home, lay off the ice cream, and be back here after school tomorrow." Coach took off his cap and rubbed his big, bald head. His pink ears stuck out like rounded fins. "And tuck in those shirts; probably be some Major League scouts hanging around looking for prospects. Don't want them to think I run a sloppy ship."

Jimmy laughed with the rest of them, then left the dugout and headed for home, just a short block down 15th Street to the Boulevard.

It still seemed strange to be walking these streets, so noisy and busy with traffic. It had only been a month since he and his dad moved here, taking a second-story apartment above the *Lindo Música Internacional* store. So many things had changed so quickly.

His parents' divorce hadn't been such a surprise; he'd figured it was coming. But he never thought his dad would be leaving Sturbridge, Pennsylvania to take a job in Jersey City. So Jimmy was left with the biggest decision of his life: stay with his mother or leave with his dad, right in the middle of seventh grade.

And here he was, suddenly a city-dweller, stuck in that urban stretch of North Jersey between the Lincoln and Holland tunnels, an arm's reach across the Hudson River from the New York City skyline. In a town where half the signs were in Spanish and white kids like him were a minority.

Exciting, but scary.

He needed to make the school baseball team. When he gripped that ball this afternoon, pushed back his cap, and peered in at the catcher, he'd finally felt at home for a few minutes. When he let loose with that wide overhand delivery and sent the ball zipping toward the plate for the first time this season, he'd felt a burden lifting.

But maybe Spencer was right. Jimmy had

been on enough sports teams to know that the coaches often did have their rosters picked way in advance, with few real opportunities for a newcomer to fit in. He'd have to do a lot better than the established players to secure a place on the team.

* * *

Rich Wallace was a high school and college athlete and then a sportswriter before he began writing novels. He is the author of many critically acclaimed sports-themed novels, including *Wrestling Sturbridge*, *Shots on Goal*, and *Restless: A Ghost's Story*. He lives with his family in Honesdale, Pennsylvania.